Green Snake

The critics have spoken...

"Laframboise does an excellent job of translating the rhythm and feel of the typical murder mystery into the realities of a snail's eye view. The story is clever and effectively conveys the point of view of the snails and the various limitations and talents available to them."

-- Robert Turner, Tangent Online, 2017

«Michèle Laframboise impresses the hell out of me. She writes beautifully in more than one genre, more than one form, and more than one language.»

-- Kristine Kathryn Rusch, Fiction River, 2017

Michèle Laframboise

Green Snake

A Case from the GGPD Files

Echofictions

Greater Garden Snail Police - 3

A WOW Story

Cover design by Echofictions
Cover pictures of snail © Michèle Laframboise
Author portrait © Gilles Gagnon
Interior illustrations by the author

This book published by : Echofictions
Mississauga, Ontario

www.echofictions.com

ISBN 978-1-988339-75-7 (print)

Table of Contents

For Josette

who loves gardens,

cats and mysteries!

Green Snake

1

TEMPERATURES IN THE GARDEN had climbed steadily since dawn, spurring a mating frenzy in the ant colonies. You could almost taste the strong formic acid odor emanating from the aggressive males along with the musky pheromones wafting off the selected females' glands. The latter were enjoying a last polishing by their sexless attendees before their maiden flight.

Of course, I couldn't see the spectacle I was describing to my class of police recruits.

All I could distinguish was a dark gleaming mass of exoskeletons covering the wide sunken slab that we were about to slime across. The slab was not natural stone, but a giant-made concrete, a mass of sand grains stuck together by a powerful glue and incredibly hard.

If I got lucky, I could get a flash of an enormous female abdomen before its long, translucid wings propelled her up in the blurry sky.

A snail's sight was average at best, and acute for rather short distances. We relied a lot on olfactive clues to assess our surroundings, which included most speech emissions.

"What do we do, officer Gowoon?" Brag asked, oozing to a stop.

He was the smallest my trainees and surprisingly fast-footed in a race, but he did not have the long-term endurance to be a messenger, like Murr.

However, he had another, non-negligible, talent.

I pulled in my smell receptors. Brag's newfound control over his pheromones tended to slip when confronted with an unexpected spectacle, like that of hundred of chitinous bodies swelling all over our path. My first impression of him had been of a braggart of the worst type, an undisciplined slogger endowed with command pheromones too powerful for his tiny shell.

The Trio reacted instantly to the mix of ants and snail pheromones. They emitted a wordless *Oooh!*, united in every way except in bodies. They were emotional sloggers, hyperreactive to any mating pheromones inadvertently released by Brag. The three were also inseparable, an advantage they had demonstrated in a recent emergency. They had been wonderfully efficient, but I wondered how they could react to carrying individual missions.

I sent the Trio a stern reminder to behave, hoping my command pheromones would get across the mating emissions of excited ants. The Trio dispelled their fantasies as soon as my molecules reached the shorter receptor stalks under their eyestalks.

Similar questions erupted from the rest of the group.

"Do we have to wait?" Murr asked, his skin exuding impatience. He was sweating profusely, as he had just carried a message to and returned from the Greater Garden Police Department HQ in a record time. I hoped he had taken time to replenish his water reserves en route. That summer promised to be hot.

"Do we have to pee?" Boon asked, his mismatched stalks waving in unison.

An accident had left him with one good eyestalk, but when signing he used both (the stump of the other moving in an awkward fashion), sending garbled messages. I did not have much hope for that one, but he behaved nicely to all other candidates. I guessed that Boon was simply echoing Murr's question.

Behind Boon, I glimpsed the scarred shell of Nool, another accident-prone slogger who generally stayed at the last place in the line. He was not a talkative type, a trait I appreciated.

Gol, the heaviest among the two-year old police candidates, oozed to a stop, his monstrous shell producing its own shade.

"They smell tasty," he emitted, his eyestalks waving hungrily at the chitinous sea.

Tip for the unwary: Big Gol was *always* hungry. Which, in the present situation, could become a problem.

"Don't even think about tasting one!" I sent.

Ants formed an organized net of underground colonies that vied for more territories.

In the present case, the path going on the side of the giant's house was occupied not by one, but two different colonies, the big glossy black ants and the small reddish ones. The two were intent to provide the maximum space for their chosen ones' nuptial flight, while doing their best to kill their competitors'.

Such a battle-com-nuptials could go on for a full morning, which was annoying. Sloggers needed to get under shade before the sun baked their shell. Waiting for the stupid ants to clear the path wasn't an option.

Problem was, in their current excited state, the ants would not respond well to our attempt to cross their path or taste their chitinous hide, as Gol proposed. They would react accordingly to what they perceive as a threat.

Lighting-fast ants, despite being tiny, could make a feast of snail meat. And, contrary to expectations, the smaller red ones were way more dangerous than the black ones.

I assessed the situation.

We were slogging mid-distance along the giant wall, covered with a layer of moving vine leaves. Our path followed a series of the slabs put in place long ago by the giants.

Giants liked to walk on those flat stones, which was a good thing, as they saved countless lives by doing so (except the stupid mating ants). The path made by those square stones started in the backyard as raised platforms. The slabs were dangerous to cross, unless you wanted to offer a meal for the birds.

As we trekked along, the slabs gradually sunk to ground level. By mid-wall, the corners of the slabs disappeared under grass, roots, and red strawberry stems. (But no yummy strawberry, alas. Their season was over.)

Ants were spilling all over the flat surface, climbing over each other in mounds that were three or four ant-bodies high.

"Ok, class, ooze down!" I called.

They crowded over the bright red strawberry stems.

"This is a perfect occasion to test your crowd control skills. We will cross that slab, forming a straight line."

Brag waved one slim eyestalk in doubt.

"In the middle of those ants?" he signed.

"Our slime trail will ward off the ants," I signed back.

Ants had the second-best olfactive sense in Garden. (The best sniffers of all being the eyeless earthworms.) Their segmented antennas would smell our presence, no way around it, but some acid in our slime was repulsive to them, so their six-packs of legs would stay clear of it.

At least, that was the theory the Chief had floated out at Headquarters. Now was the time to put it to the test.

"You, Gol, take point."

"Yessir!" he emitted, raising his foot to expose his wavering mouth. I could see his ragged teeth palettes brushing against each other. He was salivating profusely.

"No eating," I said, adding my sternest command pheromones to my emissions.

I disliked using command pheromones. First, my body had to fabricate those molecules, and the best period to do so was while at rest. Second, I was carrying a batch of eggs, which affected my command pherom's effectiveness among the hermo candidates.

"Why him?" whined Murr. "I'm the fastest."

He was right, but I detected the faint scent of sweat coming from his wrinkled skin, a tell-tale sign of exhaustion. His recent mission had tired him, but being a typical hermo, Murr was too proud to display any weakness in front of his comrades.

Except the ants would sniff out that weakness and sound the alarm. No way I would let Murr take point in his current state, pride or not.

He needed a respite, but the shelter I envisioned was two slabs away.

"You take second, in case Gol get eaten."

"What?" Big Gol exclaimed, signing with his stalks and emitting some healthy fear molecules.

I didn't want to elaborate the point, so I simply did what superior officers did, and used my authority.

"Atten-SHUT!"

All stalks stopped waving. I let a few beats pass to let go of the tension in my own skin, from the expended command pheroms. When I had their undivided attention, I gave my instructions.

"Everyone, keep your scent emissions to the lowest. I will take middle position, and make sure you behave," I added, both signing and emitting.

I turned and stretched both eyestalks to get a clearer view of the slab's farthest edge. Under the roiling mass of bodies, a spiny ridge of young thistles barred the access to the next slab. The ants waved around the spiked leaves, but we could ooze over the obstacle --and the excited ants-- without problem.

"Form a line behind Gol."

While the candidates oozed in position, I waved my receptor stalks for emphasis. "And NO emissions."

I took my position and simply oozed in front, pushing against Murr's shell, who pushed against Gol's, and that was it.

The idea of putting Gol in front was because he was the largest. We were almost swimming in his wide trail, so no ant would even come near us. And I doubted any ant trying to bite Gol would get a second chance before the candidate's large maw engulfed it.

It felt strange, so much giddy sexual emanations coming left and right, bodies wriggling this and that way, while we serenely glided among the disorder.

If I had been more disposed to signing poetry, I would wax eloquent on the symbolism of our orderly group triumphing over the chaos of unrestrained instincts.

We were three-quarter of the slab gone, according to my estimations, when my contemplative mood was cut short by a powerful burst of mindless fear.

2

ALL MY SENSES SHOT into max alert mode: smell, taste, touch, balance, sight.

My skin receptors harvested a full dose of Brag's sexy pheroms, along with acidic bursts coming from the two races of ants. They were madly scrambling over their winged chosen ones.

Then I sensed a familiar seismic jolt.

It wasn't the stomping of a rabbit scampering by, but the incredibly fast-paced feet of a giant, coming our way.

I stretched my eyestalks into tense parallel rods. Giants were so high you could only glimpse their tree-like legs, their summit losing resolution. Anyway, the giant's head would only give me useless info like the color of their eyes. I rather looked at grass-level, my stalks sweeping over the area.

Gol's big shell hid a part of the scenery. Even then, I captured a smudge of unnatural green hide moving among the grass stems. It was at least four slab-lengths distant, but the threat level had racked up a few notches. Fear emissions popped among my class.

"What's that green thingy?" One of the Trio asked.

"A monster!" Brag sent.

"A toaster?" Boon repeated, having the words garbled once more. This one would never, e-ver, work as a messenger.

"No, you fool, it's, it's the Green Snake!" Nool uttered, sending tiny puffs of panic.

In my previous tours, I had seen the Green Snake at rest, rolled over itself around a peg on the wall. My partner Zgouish had even oozed over its shiny skin and copper head, an exploit that got him a reprimand from the Chief when word of this feat got around his receptors.

Panic was spreading around us, as the familiar vibration had alerted the ants. The dark gleaming mass shivered, bodies scrambling to hurry the nuptials, wings trembling, formic acid emissions almost gagging our pneumostomes.

The Snake was on the prowl. But where was the Giant? The two events always occurred together. He must have stopped walking: no more jolt in the concrete under me. Meaning that…

I put a firm foot on my own fear and sent out short bursts of order. We had to get off that smooth, mortal surface.

"Clear the slab! To the Wall! Go, go, go!"

I set out toward the bramble of grass, strawberry, and wild roses at the wall-side edge of the slab. I went as fast as I could, sliming over one or two wayward ants on the way.

Murr oozed the fastest. Brag was pushing the slower Trio ahead of him. Nool, having been appraised of the situation, nudged on Boon to get him in the right direction. Suddenly, a pray of water droplets clogged my breathing hole. I pushed air out of my lungs to clear my pneumostome. Even short-sighted as I was, I could make out the silvery sheen of water roiling over the slab, carrying a layer of red and black bodies still moving. The hedge of thistle had slowed down the force of the tide pouring on our slab, but it was too still fast for us.

The clear water reached our line as we were hurrying toward the side. At first, the cold was a welcome sensation in the summer heat; all sloggers opened their pores to absorb the precious water inside their skin. I was no exception. But we had to reach the safer ground before the snake's head directed its powerful water jet on us.

Gol reverted to his usual reflex, splaying his wide foot down. I smelled his glue production as he was sticking himself to the slab. There was no time to explain the rookie that his strategy would only make him more visible, plus getting him crushed beneath a giant's foot.

Without losing speed, I slanted my body sideways and bumped my shell against his, hard.

"Hey!" he said.

"Inside!" I ordered.

He hadn't had the time to produce enough glue to get stuck, so he pulled his massive body inside his wide shell. Extending upward from my own foot, I gave his shell a powerful push. The layer of water made the slab slippery; I had the satisfaction of seeing Gol rolling in the right direction. But was he a load!

"Everyone, roll!" I sent.

Brag had taken the cue. He was busy nudging each shell of the Trio, one at the time, toward the edge. The Trio had unstuck themselves in as soon as Brag's strong pheromones had relayed my order. With his cracked shell, Nool couldn't imitate the others, but he pushed poor Boon's shell away with a force I could envy. The trauma of his own accident had multiplied his strength.

A vast shadow fell upon our group as the concrete slab trembled.

The giant obscured the sun as he stepped on the surface, the impact casting droplets in a wide circle. Had he done so a half-minute earlier, the whole class would have been crushed under his ponderous foot, me and my egg-pouch included. (Which would have inspired some officers at Headquarters a new rant against promoting egg-layers to investigator rank.)

The snake's copper head had risen over the horizon of grass stems, its neck clutched by a pink giant's hand. The center of our slab had become a target. The water hit the stone with such force that droplets exploded in all directions. I pulled myself inside my shell one half second before a powerful wave of water lifted me off the slab.

For dizzying moments, I careened wildly, all sense of up and down blurred, cool water clogging my pneumostome. Then, the garden stopped spinning. I waited, trusting my statocyst organ to signal that I had regain stability and balance. I extended one eyestalk to peek out from under my shell.

The wall rose over us, a plane of green oily five-foliated leaves stretching to the infinite.

The giant was not registering over the horizon anymore, but the Snake's green body was still rippling in the grass, following its master past Back Door Area, to water the vegetable patch. I was confident the sentinels posted near the cabbage patch close to the GGPD Headquarters would raise the alert and everyone one would duck for cover.

The members of my class lay a good way past the slab, amidst a bramble of twigs and leaves where the water had carried them.

I counted them, as they unrolled their bodies from their upset shells. Big Gol was already munching on tender blades of grass laced with various ant body parts. The Trio was oozing over Brag, who had, in the emotion of the moment, forgotten to stem off his sexual emissions. Fortunately, the overall moisture dripping from the grass blades where the snake had spurted water had cleaned out the dubious smells.

Murr was stretching his lean and mean foot, happy to be alive, and having replenished his water reserves sooner than anticipated. I decided to have a word in private with him, as his egoism could have cost us more sloggers. Then I berated myself. I should have instituted a buddy system before setting out. Boon was getting his one good stalk out of his shell, tentatively scanning the water-logged bramble. He was looking about for the cracked-shell buddy who had pushed him out of harm's way. In the midst of mortal danger, Nool had done a noble act.

I searched for my eighth candidate. The rookie was nowhere in my short sight. Had he rolled farther? Had the giant's foot crushed him?

I looked back at the slab we had just cleared, but a harsh white light blinded me. The glare of the sun coming off the moist quartz grains had overloaded my retinas.

I sent out a scented signature call, which was picked up and relayed by the others. It was the usual GGPD protocol for locating a missing patrol member. Brag's powerful scent emitters augmented the reach of the collective call, while I kept my receptors open.

We waited, long minutes while the pitiless sun crossed over the giant's wall.

No answer reached our group.

The gallant Nool had not made it.

*

The Trio huddled together, a lumpy yellow-orange mass oscillating on the unequal ground. Each of those young sloggers was realising how it could have been one of them missing. The siblings had grown close since they hatched.

Brag was mourning in his own way, babbling non-stop to Gol about his exploits, like the race he had finished ahead of a seasoned officer (he had cheated, but now was not a good moment to set the record straight.) The big rookie did not give Brag's spinning stalks any attention, busy as he was munching on a mix of greens and dead ants, his sharp-teeth radula rolling the food inside his vast curling mouth.

Sloggers normally did not eat insects, but there were exceptions. GGPD officers had to survive in dire situations. I still remember the horribly spicy taste of a dead wasp, from my own training tour. I had kept the translucent wings for last, as they tasted like stale pollen.

An acrid mourning scent came my way.

Boon's lone eyestalk waved as he oozed over the twigs, sending a salutation that was probably a frantic call.

I couldn't let my class mull on the loss any longer. The Snake's body had stopped moving about., meaning the giant was busy watering the Headquarters neighborhood. I hoped my usual partner Zgouish had found a cover. I did not fear for the Chief, as his underground office under the maple counted several evacuation tunnels. Even with a good rain, water would pass in the lower burrows (meaning the Medic Examiner's labs) before trickling out through the roots.

I called formation. Time to go and forget that darn snake.

All in all, losing only one candidate were better odds than I expected.

3

WE SLOGGED in a parallel line to the slab path, passing the now-silent battlefield. Red and black chitinous hides cracked under my foot, antennas protruding like twigs. Ants of both species had been washed down and away, releasing an acrid smell of decay and moist leg hair. The sun was baking our carbonaceous shells.

Quick, darting shadows obscured the light for a split second. Birds were about, looking for lunch. Poor Boon emitted a sharp tingle of fear scent and whipped inside his shell so fast it wobbled.

Worm dung! The loss of Nool must have rattled him.

Boon's reflex had been a good one, because sloggers shells were quite hard for most predator's teeth. But the bigger birds had learned how to pick up a shell in their claws and let it drop on from a high altitude on the hard stones. While investigating a missing slogger case, I had happened upon the resulting mess, a mental image I wished to spare my class.

I banged on his shell, using side moves of my own. A creamy membrane was forming on his shell's opening, a protective epiphragm that cut everything (even odors) from him. Sealing himself, even if it was deemed acceptable on a hot summer day, was a no-no in the GGPD. Cutting oneself from the rich well of scent information delayed any investigation. Plus, it was the equivalent of offering one's body as a meal for the savvier birds.

I opened my maw and bit off the membrane, ignoring its moldy taste. When Boon's lone eyestalk moved in the shadow (he had squeezed his body real hard against the curved walls of his shell, dangerously squishing his organs in the process), I sent some choice words to the cowering candidate.

"Garden patrol isn't all roses and tender roots! Get out!"

There was a time to be nice, and a time to show tough love.

"Shit happens," I said. "Death is all around us, and most of it is revolting, and unjust. This was why you wanted in." I made a large stalk circle to include the assembled candidates sniffing on our conversation.

Another shadow flitted overhead, so low I glimpsed its feathered belly. Speaking of death... We had to get out of the sun. In the dampened grass, our striped shells shone like lunch beacons.

"But the GGPD has no place for wimps in its ranks," I sent, summoning my best command pheroms. "If you want to become an officer, you have first to live!"

That shook him, because his eyestalk, then shorter receptor stalks emerged from the shell.

"On the move! All in line behind me."

Taking the point, I oozed closer to the wall. More shadows zoomed over, small crisp contours. I glided along, keeping a calm demeanour that I was far from feeling.

My shell was heating up so much that my lung, compressed against the inner wall, felt the strain. Only my recent intake of water from the Snake helped me cope.

Those kind of death claws were less dangerous that the big, white flapping ones who were crafty enough to know the trick of breaking our shell.

And there were the tortoises. Their beak was so powerful it could crunch our shell, like soft mud. Fortunately, the last one had left the Greater Garden Area last fall. According to the Chief, there was a big forest, some jurisdictions over, where predators roamed loose.

A dangerous place, he had said, having lived there before coming to our Garden and battling for the territory.

Finally, I felt a welcoming shadow, and smelled the cement and leaves mix of the wall's base. The extended leaves of the vine would provide cover while we waited out the scorching heat.

4

THE UNEXPECTED WATERING had spread water on the wall vines that were dripping over us. Everything was pleasantly moist.

As my class sucked that life-replenishing moisture inside, I noticed a crowd forming. Not the ants, even if another colony (or was it the same?) was busy sending their chosen up, legs and antennas quivering, reddish torsos emitting a lusty acrid scent. They merely receded from our approach.

An assortment of Garden citizens lived at the wall base, mostly one-cyclers, not the sharpest minds about. Our line gathered much attention from the locals, attention which quickly turned into defiance as the GGPD badges inscribed on our shells registered, either by sight or scent.

On that last subject, I had to remind my class to lick up their badge, so the scent signature of the GGPD would be kept fresh. This was a reason why the mark was etched on the side of our shell, an easy reach. Only Gol, mouth always full, experienced some difficulties in basic uniform maintenance.

Wall was not by any stretch the worst of Garden neighborhoods; that palm went to Basement, a place under the Giant's shelter where lots of food, beer and mayhem occurred among the low lives gathered there. I had been there once and didn't plan to return any time soon.

"Hey, there's something there!" Gol said, his height giving him a better view of our environment.

His stalks were pointing toward a crowd of one-year-old nameless sloggers, three or four body-lengths from our position. Those had been born last autumn, contrary to my class born in the previous spring. Their shell was only beginning to show the pale swirling violet marks that would darken during their first winter hibernation into a unique, personalized pattern.

They were in those early stages of learning by mistakes (or not learning anything and piling on the mistakes until a death claw put an end to it).

They were also very vulnerable to suggestion, which often made them targets of hardened criminals. If you needed a messenger or a carrier for your stolen goods, ask a first-cycler barely hatched from the egg.

I made an educated guess that the two thirds of that crowd would be gone before the end of the summer.

Nevertheless, they had learned to get on the shade to escape the heat, so maybe I was letting my paranoid nature get the better of me. Those sloggers were Garden citizens, and as such, entitled to police protection. I had a passing thought for the hatchling that my class of candidates had pulled off the beer trap this morning.

Oozing into the crowd, my shell brushed against smaller shells. The smooth-shelled sloggers immediately made room for me, letting me see the immobile form at the center. For a horrible, guilt-ridden moment, I though it was the poor Nool, but no, the body was different, longer, and without a shell.

"Is that a crime scene?" Brag sent, interrupting my thoughts. His molecules bore a little too much excitement, unbecoming for a GGPD officer. Most of the class was echoing the question.

I sent a stern *restrain your emissions!* order.

The Trio unlocked from their collective hug, Boon rose his lone eyestalk at attention, Gol stopped munching. He had found a dried-up and shrivelled strawberry, its decaying smell revived by the giant's watering. I twisted my head back to the assembly.

Before checking if the body was still warm or cold, I extended my receptors stalks and opened my mouth wide.

It was an essential component of an investigation to get the most of a crowd's emissions. Especially before proceeding to a formal interrogation. The Chief always said that first impressions counted in a case.

I registered morbid curiosity, fear, a subdued mating request (the discovery of the body had stopped at least one nuptial parade), and aimless anguish puffs so typical of first cyclers, all enrobed in a bubble of disquiet.

I dismissed the anguished puffs, a normal part of growing pains. I also dismissed the morbidly curious, another kind of growing-up experience. None of those small shells could have killed that worm.

The earthy scent had of the skin had told me the vic was not a slogger. I needed to examine the body, but the crowd felt little inclined to leave the premises.

Nevertheless, this was a learning occasion. I ordered my class to take their SOC positions. A scene of crime had to be protected until a qualified investigator like yours truly completed the examination.

"And remember your crowd control instructions!" I said, as the smaller shells crowded ours.

"But, it's only a dirty worm!" Murr said, his skin releasing disgust. "Why make a SOC?"

So much for 'refraining', I thought.

Really, Murr's attitude would have to be corrected if I wanted to present him for the officer nomination. Worms were my favorite indicators, and even the Chief had accepted my use of their expertise.

"Worms, despite being "dirty" (my short acrid burst put an emphasis on the intended slur) possess the most discriminating smell sense of all Greater Garden."

This did not appease the class: half of it had taken Murr's position.

"But they're so stupid/idiot/thoughtless!" the Trio emitted together, their scent signals overlapping to create a slight discordance.

"They don't even have eyes" Brag added, his cloying emission dragging the trio's short-span attention on him.

That had been the chief's and the ME objections, too. Idiots, eyeless worms couldn't make reliant informers.

"I admit earthworms are not the most intellectual beings in garden, and their use as informants has its drawbacks. But the quality of the tips they can give, providing you know how to get their attention, upsets any disadvantages."

I let my class mull on the succession of scent notes I just released on them. Talking in emissions could get tiresome, so I resorted to my eyestalks to complete the lesson.

As I was finishing giving instructions, I noticed one shell-less slug hurrying away from the crowd, toward the vertical wall. Slugs were the anathema of proper garden citizens, eyeless and shell-less. Maybe I entertained my own prejudices against them after my Basement experience last spring.

Anyway, this slug looked like he wanted to keep his scent emissions from the police. I tensed my eye and receptors in his direction, while sending a puff of command pheromones.

"Class, arrest this slug!"

5

THERE WERE NO NICETIES to be respected while patrolling, so the candidates heaved and pulled and advanced in the wake of the receding slug.

The move was definitively not an orderly one. Big Gol slimed over one or two yearlings (fortunately, not inflicting lasting damage as the smaller snails were squeezed off sideways). Murr disputed the lead to Brag, the Trio going strong on their tails. The slime trails multiplied, sending a few scarabs fluttering away.

I left the group of tightly packed shells speeding away to concentrate on the body.

Its was a big-sized individual, reaching more than four body-lengths. This size let me estimate its age at four-year-old. It was a feat in Garden to survive that long, as worms got a lot of predators eager to gobble them. No wonder they preferred to stay underground, despite the other dangers lurking there.

I took a sniff off its still-moist skin. I was immediately reminded about a stormy night, pounding rain and white flashes revealing the soft grey underbelly of clouds. My foot rippled slowly as a pang of sadness overtook me.

One of my best informers lay there.

*

THAT WORM HAD NO NAME, but its signature would be always associated for me with basement, and storm.

Most worms were rather short-minded, deeply afraid the death claws that could rip them off the protective layer of soil. The older ones, by surviving longer, had developed a limited consciousness of Garden. They knew more about stuff going around, even if they didn't understand all of it, like for instance our craving for yeast, or why a beer trap constituted a serious peril for sloggers.

Sliming around my informer's annulated body, I searched for the cause of death. Normally, this would be the medical examiner's job, but all hands at Headquarters would be busy staving off the watering. (Plus, I hated his guts and the feeling was reciprocal.)

I inched closer. The worm had a gob of soil stuck in its toothless mouth.

Usually, any soil particle travelled through the whole body and its digested remains exited at the back. Their action on the soil were generally appreciated by all inhabitants. I checked around, looking for the hole from which that worm had gotten out of. And did not find one in eyesight. I tried to sniff out its trail, but the snake's aspersion had left a water layer that diluted his tracks. That worm could as well have materialized here.

Pushing back my aversion, I checked the worm's other end. I saw a hard rusty-looking piece stuck in the anus. The angular piece had been small enough to travel through the worm's bowels. I detected a metallic odor, not at all like organic excrements mixed with sand grains that I would have expected. I extended one stalk to touch the reddish metal, probably iron. Giants used a lot of metals: iron, silver, copper, cadmium, most easy to find in the ground.

My receptor stalk had barely made contact that I reeled back from shock. It wasn't rusting iron at all.

Pure copper.

The toxic metal must have traveled in the worm's elongated stomach and intestines, sending its metal ions to nestle in the soft tissues. The weight of my carbonaceous shell seemed to press down on my body. My informer had died of food poisoning. It happened in Garden, but something here was amiss. My former informer would never eat a pure metal piece. Such an acute poisoning couldn't have been an accident.

I checked the gob in the worm's mouth. I shook it off, using not my mouth, of course, but my foot's edge. It looked like a usual clay particle. I pressed on it: the clay cracked, revealing another rusty-looking piece. A coppery smell rose from the exposed object.

A cold realisation dripped under my shell.

Murder.

The most probable scenario was that someone (the slug?) had advertised a tip, using clay-enrobed gobs as baits. Able to absorb small quantities of the metal naturally present in the ground, the old worm would have smelled the presence of copper. Except that the layers of clay had masked its unusual concentration.

Normally, I would produce some glue to affix the cleaned gob to my shell. But I would have to touch it directly, a contact I did not care for. I was fiercely protective of the eggs maturing inside me; any metal in my metabolism would hinder their development.

I left the body and its poison onsite to follow the slime trail of my class.

If the candidates came back with the slogger of interest bound to Big Gol's shell, I would be happy to demonstrate our interrogation techniques. (Not for the faint of heart, those. A slobbering "kiss of death" administered by an experienced officer could reduce the meanest thug to a whimpering mass.)

A pursuit in Garden did not hold the same excitement as inside the giant's magic box that Zgouish and I had spied on while carrying a special mission ordered by the Chief. (Ascending the south wall in the evening was fraught with danger, but the occasion to sit on a windowsill near my hunky partner had been worth the trouble. I couldn't differentiate the moving forms on the box's surface, but Zgouish had the better sight.)

I hurried on, absorbing as much moisture as I could on the way.

We were going northward, which was good, as the recruit's Training Tour covered all of Garden territories. Alas, soon, I found out that the slug had diverted his path out of the protective shade of the lower vine leaves.

There was only a narrow band of soil between the slab's edge (where the ants had moved their nuptials) and the wall. The grass there was uneven, patchy, rife with dandelions and asters. Large areas of bare soil would expose a clutter of shells, especially as said shells would be shiny from a recent dousing.

As I was thinking this, a shock registered through my foot.

Then another.

The case just got more complicated.

6

A GIANT WAS AMBLING from the south. Transmitted by the concrete slabs, the powerful vibration of his steps shook the packed earth I was gliding on. I twisted my upper body to look behind me, extending my eyestalks.

Sure enough, giant's legs were approaching at this incredible pace, the upper body towering over the green horizon. I had thought the bipedal had finished his business with the snake.

I sent an acid warning signal to the class, hoping the breeze would carry it to them. Giant's Coming was the first warning signal police candidates learned. Odors expanded faster that giant's footsteps, so the class would have some time to scatter away.

The stupid ants, blinded by their mating frenzy, were still carrying on their nuptials, en masse. I did not need a bird's eye to picture them blanketing the slabs. All hopeless except, maybe, their well-hidden queen. Only their sheer numbers protected ants from a host of competitors.

The giant approached my position. I retracted partially under my shell, offering the least visible surface.

I tensed my eyestalks in a parallel disposition to register a maximum of input. The giant's legs were covered with sparse fur; they disappeared under a cottony fabric moving along. The upper body and head were a blur. Only Zgouish's sight could discriminate a giant's head (with more fur on the top, he had told me).

I pointed both stalks mid-height, and hit pay dirt.

The Green Snake moved along with the giant.

The giants' pink claws had gripped its shiny head, clear droplets dripping from its snout. It was not gushing water anymore. I guessed that the cabbage patch and Headquarters had been thoroughly drenched. Officers would be counting bodies and reporting to the Chief's upper office.

The giant's other paw clutched a small shiny rectangle. Then he lifted it out of my sight. According to Zgouish, giants held the rectangle against their curved vibration receptors. Chief said they communicated by another sense that sloggers didn't possess.

The giant cleared the sky, trailing the snake's body behind him. I surmised that, as I slogged along, I would eventually find the snake rolled on its peg. I watched its body sliding over the slab, covered with dirt and gobs of clay.

Then, it stopped moving.

I hurried on. Usually, the giant rolled the entire snake on its peg, leaving the snout hanging free. I waited until the vibration of his footsteps receded. The green snake still lay there. There was no understanding of those beings, even if some patterns repeated themselves, like their watering schedule.

While my foot rippled over fallen twigs to reach my class, I twisted my head south and opened my skin receptors. Endowed with the third-best sense of smell after the worms and the ants, I identified the odor of moist cabbages, along with very faint callings from GGPD officers. The situation back there was under control, so I reported my attention to the north.

Following the trail scent, I encountered earth-smelling containers lined down, forcing me to pass between the wall and their round base. I knew what I would find on the other side: the snake's resting place. When I got out off the shadow, I spotted my group of candidates. They were scattered on the slab, next to a tall cliff that reached all the way to a giant's door.

My recruits were soaked, but alive.

7

THE SIDE DOOR was an active place for giants, with the snake-less peg and containers. I felt grateful that the giant had not noticed the congregation of various shells, especially big Gol's, almost on their doorstep. Something else must have distracted him, as he had not even pulled the snake back on its peg. I wonder if he was still using the shiny rectangle.

The snake itself was most probably lying somewhere among the tall grass blades. Giant things were strangers to reason.

Whatever, my class had survived. It would normally have been a cause for celebration, but the murder weighted on my mind. I led my class off that slab and closer to the line of smelly containers, where young dandelion sprouts would conceal our presence.

Later, I checked each candidate for wounds, finding none. However, my relief was short-lived: there was no prisoner to interrogate.

No slug had been attached to their shell. I cast and tensed my receptor stalks, to no avail. A slug stench was normally easy to follow. How could it have disappeared so fast?

"Report," I sent.

There was a lot of foot-shifting and stalk-waving around. I cast my question again, both stalk-signing and skin-emitting. I had emptied my command pheroms with the Giant's warning, but my request passed in a strong puff.

"Where did that slug go?"

More foot-ripples, eyestalks waving in loose circles.

Finally, Brag oozed forward, his foot undulating in a one-two rhythm, the pace of shame.

"The perp got away," he said.

I had gathered as much. I used to use this failure as an object lesson. Despite Brag's contrite position, I sent a stern warning.

"First of all," I signed, "even if that slug was fleeing the crime scene, you do NOT call it a "perp". The right term is "witness" or "slogger of interest".

"But a slug is not a real slogger," one candidate – Murr, of course - protested.

"Silence, class! I'm not finished."

That last outburst used up a fair amount of my reserves. I felt grateful to have absorbed water slogging here. When I was certain their emissions were under control, I pursued.

"In the Greater Garden jurisdiction, there's a presumption of innocence until proven guilty. As far as we know, that slug hasn't perpetrated a crime. Unless one of you actually witnessed the murder."

I moved one eyestalk in tiny circles, an outward sign of reflection.

The pause served to help the notion sink under their shell and, hopefully embed in the part of the four-chamber brain sitting there. I kept my other eyestalk on every recruit's foot, checking the patterns. Most candidates had slowed down their rippling but Murr hadn't. He was still mulling about the reprimand.

"If you had caught the witness, we would then proceed to interrogation. Then, if the witness' alibi can be verified, we let him free."

"But how can you know if he lied?" one of the Trio asked.

I suppressed my surprised reaction because the Trio was usually more intent on mating than listening. So, they were also able to think by themselves, without Brag urging them.

Good.

"In the GGPD, we have… ways of detecting liars," I signed.

It took seasons to affine our smell senses to detect the acidic sweat of a liar. This was my own very personal skill, a skill which had got me the best crime-solving rate of the GGPD. Some jealous colleagues argued that my being an egg-layer had somehow heightened my sensitivities. Hence their maneuvering to put me in charge of the recruit patrol.

Whatever.

For now, I preferred that the candidates ignore my liar-detector skill. First, I did not want to display my sexual specifics to a band of hermos. Second, they could get discouraged when learning how long it took to master the skills. Some four or five-year-old officers never did.

The Trio ahhed and ooohed at my answer. Gol shrugged, which let me see his clogged respiratory hole.

"For now, you're better clean your pneumostome if you want to be able to smell tracks," I sent, my stalks pointing to the concerned candidate.

Gol twisted his big body and set to task with his stalks.

"This applies to all of you," I added.

As they were busy cleaning their orifices, I pursued. A spicy-scented brown ball drifted from above. Aster plants shoot up from the slab's interstices, their pink petals open. "You will notice, class, about the aster pods. Their smells are often used by criminal elements to mask their scent."

Of course, the Trio fell upon the lone pod, eager to taste that junk food. It took Gol's big foot and my stern command to get them to behave. My new-found admiration for the Trio members waned.

"What about the slug?" Brag asked. "We lost its trail so fast."

"Yeah," Murr added, a touch of scorn in his emissions. "They're so stinky, it's a wonder how we could lose it."

I thought about it. Slugs were marginally faster that snails. But none could evade a band of police officers in training, not with two fast sloggers among them. I looked again at the lone pod, its spicy scent playing with my other smells.

"This one must have found a hiding spot out with a strong scent, enough to cover it."

Around us, the bramble was full of underground passages, ants evac exits, and the occasional, unnaturally straight hole dug by the giants. Not counting the aligned containers' moist undersides and the vine stems interlacing on the wall.

"Scatter and search!"

The class oozed around, searching the loose soil with its assortments of refuse, roots, and leaves. A few black ants wove their way, which told me that the big mating event had been interrupted.

I checked on the sun's position. The afternoon was coming. It seemed we would have to spend the hot hours at the wall's base.

A call echoed from Boon, coming from behind a container.

"Found it!"

I slogged over, my sides rippling fast. When the others joined me, I saw Boon oozing back and forth, aster pods dotting the mix of sand and clay eroded from the wall. I did not need to sniff out the pungent aster smell to conclude that any useful clue would be gone. The fleeing witness had stretched thin to slither down a crevice, or under the ponderous containers.

Brag was stretching himself to squeeze under.

"Must be there," he sent.

I sent an order.

"Get out."

Undersides were the territory of roaches. If the slug was there, no way our shells could pass under.

"But what do we do?" Brag said.

"We get back the way we came."

At least, I would have something to explain the class, and Big Gol could carry the copper grain without fearing contamination.

"But we're tired," Boon said, his lone stalk waving.

I cut through his lamentation.

"You're not tired, you're a GGPD officer."

I led the way.

"Onward," I said. "And stick to the wall."

As we ambled on, a familiar scent wafted to me. I twisted an eyestalk behind. Sure enough…

"Gol," I sent, "I didn't mean that last order literally!"

The big candidate was trying to glue himself to the vertical cement wall.

8

WE MADE GOOD TIME, using the vines as cover against the harsh sun. The Trio complained loudly they needed to estivate. No way: GGPD officers had to learn to master their instincts when presented with their duty.

When we got back to the crime scene, a nasty surprise was waiting for us.

The worm's body had disappeared.

I slogged through the area. No clue presented itself. I couldn't even sniff the copper grain around. However, I observed a dozen of tiny parasites wriggling in the sandy soil. The kind of critters that were at home in a bird's feathers...

Of course! I thought, mentally assessing the time elapsed since the discovery. There were a host of birds checking on the ant's nuptials. A big fat worm would be a gift.

"A hungry death claw took it," I said.

The bird's sweeping wings would have sent my tiny copper proof far away. Great.

A dispirited feeling oozed over my normally sharp mind.

Good, reliable informants were difficult to come by. Most worms were stupid, hungry and sex craved. Only the bigger individuals, having gained more life experience along with body mass, proved themselves useful.

That loss sent me in a dark mood spiral.

The modus operandi told me that the big worm had been expertly assassinated. Which meant a new criminal group had moved on to take up the beer trafficking.

That informant's murderer had gotten away scot-free, using the snake as a distraction. Even the slug must have been a red herring, as the poisoning could have occurred anytime in the night before.

By erasing all odors, the water had provided a clean slate for the murderer. And, while we were pursuing the slug, that poor worm's body had gone down the gullet of a bird.

"So," Brag said, "what do we do now?"

My class was good, but far from ready to investigate such a highly sophisticated crime.

"Nothing," I said. "Except preparing a report."

Murr made a rolling motion, exuding impatience.

"A report? What for?" he asked.

Anger crafted a red mist around my vision field. I turned from Murr to encompass the whole bunch of candidates.

"That's what you do, class, when you lose the trail!"

I may have left some anger seep through my signals, because the whole class flowed back, leaving a sparkling slime circle.

What a drag! We were used to giant's interference with normal police business, but this one took the ripe strawberry! Criminal elements had found a way to use the giants against the GGPD! And I needed to get a stalk-to-stalk conversation with eager Murr and snarky Brag.

If, as I suspected, a new criminal gang had moved on, I needed to send a report ASAP to Headquarters. I summoned Murr for the task. That would get him out of my foot for a while.

After I sent him on his way, with stern order not to stop until he reached headquarters, there was nothing else to do. I allowed the class to retire inside their shell and estivate to pass the hot midday hours, provided they kept under the cover of vines. As they were salivating to produce the mucus to seal their shell entrance shut, I offered to take the first watch.

For once, no one had the energy to complain.

9

I LOOKED OVER THE QUIET GROUP of shells. While the candidates were happily dreaming of crisp lettuce leaves and horny encounters, I set out to work.

What I had to do needed the utmost privacy. I searched the area for a safe place. I found what I needed, a moist patch of ground under a wide leafy plant. I used my foot to scatter sand away, burrowing a hole one shell-length deep.

Then, I sat on it, extending my oviduct. I could feel by whole foot rippling with a mix of joy and sorrow as a hundred of tiny white balls fell from the end.

There were two good reasons for me to lay my eggs now, not far from the crime scene. First, the criminal elements would avoid the place for a good period, leaving my eggs alone. Second, I needed to be free of any descendance inside me as I would conduct the training sessions in dangerous territory. Front Yard district was way more dangerous that backyard. No way I would risk my clutch out there.

Snails were not good at parenting like birds (and would you imagine a bird feeding a hundred hungry mouths?) We usually laid eggs in a hole, made sure they would be OK, and forgot about them. I salivated to cover the soft white balls with a mucus layer that would protect them from harm.

They would never know me and vice-versa, but some hatchlings, like the inseparable Trio, tended to stay together for life.

I expelled from my own shell some grains of the giants' white calcareous sand, the powder they put in garden to counter acidity of the soil. A few well-read GGPD officers had taken the habit to add extra-calcium in their egg caches, to give their young a better chance at surviving their hatching.

Freshly hatched sloggers' shells were soft at first; they had to harden their shell to survive outside. Most did so by eating their egg mates when there was no other source of calcium nearby.

I had been hoarding calcareous grains under my shell for several days.

Releasing the powdery grains over my eggs made me feel proud that I had gone to great lengths for them. I extended my receptors and eyestalks downward, taking in their wonderful, egg-filled smell, breathing their tiny lives in my lung. I would record their scent signature to recognize them once they hatched, which would be later this summer, or in fall. Not all sloggers cared to remember their young's scents.

But then, not all had been endowed with a very well-honed sense of smell, nor had they trained this gift into a sharp investigating tool. The tool that allowed me to rise in the ranks of the GGPD.

Again, I gazed at my clutch with pride. I poured sand over the tiny balls, sending a last puff of *goodbye* and *good luck*.

Then, it was all. I oozed away. I couldn't do anything more.

Relieved, I set to estivate close to my class, keeping a tiny part of my own shell opened to the world.

10

THE PATTERN OF LIGHT AND SHADOW on my operculum, along with the temperatures cooling, rose me from a sound sleep. I ate the thin, crisp membrane and oozed out of my shell, satisfied that most of the candidates were barely stirring.

While they went through the moves of de-estivating, I slogged to the edge of the covering to assess the weather.

The cloudless sky had turned into an aggressive hue. The sun had moved. By now, the giant's house's shadow covered the side and front yard. Most sloggers would become active at dusk, but we had a good road ahead, and I wanted to pass the snake's peg and side door before the giants rose from their own estivation.

I oozed on without letting my class finish to emerge. It was a subtle way to impose my authority because they would have to scramble to catch up with me.

The distance between the crime scene and the side door was shorter than I had thought at first. The afternoon temperature had barely changed when we went in view of the snake's peg.

There as no snake on it, even if its tail was staunchly fixed to another, lower peg on the wall. The class had reformed the line behind me.

"Where's the green snake?" Boon asked, his lone eyestalk inquiring.

Logically, somewhere in the grass nearby.

"Follow the lead," I said, in a snarky puff of derision, one stalk extended toward the snake's body disappearing among the high grass stems. Not that I expected anyone to comply, least of all Boon.

But Gol took the lead, his obstinacy, or willingness to obey, remarkable.

I urged my shell ahead, catching up to the big candidate before he followed the green tubular body. That was when I noticed the snake was resting over several loops, its sides still caked with mud. I pictured the giant looping its green length, intent to hang it back on the peg. Then some other rampage must had called him forth before his finished the task.

That was the danger with giants: their abrupt change of ideas, which made their behavior difficult to predict. Not like the ants.

The snake kept still, its head low to the ground, the water-spitting snout, a black hole that seemed to fascinate Gol.

"Don't go near it," I said.

"Smells good," he said. "Familiar."

I couldn't believe what he could find familiar here, so I rose my upper body and smacked his shell sideways. It took some doing because his shell was bigger than mine.

"Get back," I said.

He complied, while the rest of the group had made a loose circle to sample the food around.

I had ordered the group to form a new line and follow me when a strong, sensual emission kicked a thousand tiny worms inside me.

"Mind if I butt in?"

*

THE TRIO'S STALKS tensed in the direction of the scented message. I didn't need to turn, as I had recognized the sexy pheromones of my partner.

Zgouish oozed into sight, a big, sturdy hunk that made my heart go *boing!* His scarred shell was so impressive even Big Gol looked up from his food.

His powerful foot muscles rippled in a most alluring way. He must have run from Headquarters, but he did not exhibit the least trace of exhaustion. Zgouish was an accomplished athlete and officer. Standing there, huffing and sweating, Murr was taking the full measure of his own bragging.

"The Chief got your report and sent me," he signed. "So, a new criminal band has moved in?"

Before I could answer, a wordless, primal mating burst tore me from my partner.

"Oooooh!" The Trio oozed on, their bodies waving in a 2-4 tempo ripple, their released pheroms in perfect accord.

An anguished call wafted from another direction. Brag was waving his stalks to and fro, from the Trio to my hunky partner.

Zgouish had so much sex-appeal that he had drew the Trio's full attention. Brag cast off all self-control and expelled a stymied flow of sexual pheroms toward his usual acquaintances. The trio made no notice of his antics as they continued to advance toward Zgouish, their sides fluttering with lust, their slimy trail shining.

Poor Brag. For once, the snarky slogger's incredible capacities proved useless.

For the first time in his short life, he was utterly ignored. Even his most romantic emissions were dispelled by Zgouish's masterful pheromones.

Then, under the placid vine leaves, Brag made his move. He oozed forward, his sides were flowing in an angry 4-8 pattern towards my partner. Of course, Zgouish picked up Brag's aggressive stance and raised his head in a ritual display of strength. This was a slugfest in the making. Unless, of course, the two of them mated, as some slugfests ended. Which was worse?

Chief should have chosen someone else to carry his message. Unless...

Unless it hadn't been the venerable Chief, but the crafty, sneaky Medical Examiner who had chosen the messenger. (The ME and I had sparred in the recent past, he trying to mate at inconsiderate times. He resented my presence in the GGPD, but my own olfactive prowess had proved invaluable to the Chief. So, there I was.)

Problem was, I, their superior officer, sat squat in the middle of their little emission war. Any moment, I would either twist myself around Zgouish in a torrid and uncensored fluids exchange or roll over little Brag (out of pity, of course). Worm dung, I thought.

Letting my animal brain take the relay would do more than hinder this investigation, it would jettison my entire career in the police.

One of the tenets of patrolling the Garden was clear: no intimate relationships on the job. (Off-hours and in one's own warm burrow were another thing, however.) Plus, engaging in hot steamy sex in front of my recruits would dispel any authority I had painfully managed to garner. My class would be lost, unless Zgouish took the lead from yours truly.

Of course, by mating with me, my partner would be punished for breaking discipline. As a result, my class, with no one to take it and shape it, would be lost. Let alone in the harsh environment of the front yard, they would quickly get killed.

I felt my foot rippling on its own accord.

As a hazy bubbling mayhem rose in my brain, I decided that if I was to lose my control, better it be with little Brag, instead of Zgouish. I would get sacked, and maybe Brag would, too. But at least, my friend and partner would still have his career in the GGPD. My class would have a worthy instructor to see them through the rest of their training. And I would have more free time to find a safe spot to lay the eggs growing in me.

With luck, Brag would be spared, as his young age and slight built could excuse him. As a medium-sized three-year old, I could force myself on a smaller one.

In theory only. I had never, e-ver considered forcing someone else before.

But those weren't normal circumstances, my addled part countered. And cute little Brag would not be totally unwilling to comply, given his accelerating 4-8 rippling.

My, my, wasn't he a chunky little snail!

That's when my left eyestalk caught a metallic reflection. The snake head! The clear and present danger chased off any sexual urge I may have felt.

I sent a frantic alarm call… that went unheeded by the contenders. Brag's speed would give him an advantage against Zgouish. The two could engage in a death battle for me. As romantic as the idea seemed, the end result would not be helpful at all.

Then, an idea struck me. I elongated my body to get a better view. The sun had baked the grass, letting me see the tubular metal head at rest. The snake was rolled on its peg on the wall, at repose. But its mortal spout was turned in our direction.

I oozed away from the contenders and the circle of locals that the imminent slugfest had drawn. Distractions were rare near the wall.

I had observed the snake, long enough to form a theory about its inner workings. The snake, I gathered, was like any container: hollow. The way water gushed from it, there was some pressure, like when the ants projected their formic acid. Logically, there must be some obstruction that kept the water inside, that the giant's hand could dislodge. And, as logically, put it back in place.

It took all my courage to slog past a few yearlings tasting desire for their first time, and to reach the round mouth of the snake.

Death by drowning loomed in my mind like a dark storm cloud. But, if my plan worked, there would be no dying.

And no unregulated mating.

11

I SLOGGED OVER THE VILE COPPER, oozing to find the spot that the giant had touched. The metal felt inordinately cool, confirming my theory about the water coursing through his body, like blood and slime.

The snake had a kind of collar terminating its tubular body. On that collar, a branch extended, half as long as the head.

I pictured the giant's mighty hand clutching the branch. The branch had moved, toward the head. Water had gushed out.

That was it! Now, if only I could pull the branch. Zgouish would have been perfect for the task, but once involved in a slugfest, nothing else existed for him. Even at this distance, I could smell the sharp, tangy excitement in the air.

No mating had taken place yet, no love darts launched yet, as Brag's angry release and Zgouish's mocking replies made plain. There was a chance to make things right, provided I was fast enough.

And provided I made enough glue.

I sighed inwardly. (And outwardly, but no one would smell my emissions.) Glue was another pedagogic item on my list that would get ignored by my excited and squirming recruits. Police officers underwent severe training to fabricate glue in record time. They also learned the lawful use this tool.

Projected gobs of fast-drying glue had stopped many perps. I thought about the lone slug fleeing the scene. No time to slime after it, but I could sniff the trail later, when everyone had calmed down. Tracking a suspect would provide a useful education to the class.

Stranded on the Snake's head, I oozed and oozed, producing the best glue I could.

12

FOR ALL ITS TOXICITY, the copper behaved marvellously, sticking fast. It was a strange paradox that I would feel thankful for the Snake's spraying, as it had allowed me to replenish my water reserves.

Once the glue at the base of my foot had solidified, I extended my upper body toward the branch, which I grabbed by my eyestalks.

This tight curving around a hard object provoked a queer dizziness in my sight, but it did not faze me. I knew to rely on my olfactive receptors and my cytostatic organ to get the mental picture of my surroundings. Stalks were underrated for use in close combat, as they were delicate and easy to chomp on. However, they had a fair resistance to linear tension.

I concentrated my strength into the pulling, picturing a long rest in my comfy shell once that exercise was over. I contracted my belly muscles, a sheen of slime oozing out by every pore of my stretched skin.

Nothing moved. The branch did not even budge.

As the smells of the cheering crowd told me, I had only minutes to act.

Despair brushed my shell. I would not be able to do it. I would lose the class to shenanigans.

"May I?" someone offered, sending up a puff of goodwill and tasty chives.

I expulsed a cloud of instructions. Munching, Big Gol took position beside me. He had already glued himself to the cool copper, faithful to his survival strategy. He stretched, and his mouth seized the bar.

We pulled. I felt my stalks thickening, as the lever gave way. Then…

The snake awoke.

Its head wove right and left, as the jet of water, so fast it looked to me as a trembling silver cord, struck the crowd. Devious, sexy emissions were instantly dispelled, their molecules chased across the next slab. The snake's head shook us to get rid of us, but we stood fast. When I could not endure more painful stretching, I let go of the bar, sending a feeble "Follow me" order to the hefty candidate.

I felt myself roll into my shell as I flew by, one eye catching separate images of the crowd dispersing. My shell struck the bramble close to the former rivals.

Slender strawberry stems shook as Gol's shell landed on them.

I sent a "Assemble" signal. The bramble had been waterlogged, but when we let go of the branch, the snake had stopped spouting water.

Zgouish was extending his stalks in the look-afar manoeuvre that I had not mastered yet, taking in the copper head. His sensuous lip waved in a crooked smile.

"Wow. This is a first in Garden. How did you stop the Green Snake?"

The compliment almost rocked me off my foot. But pride swelled in me.

"The snake looks like an animal, but it is no more than another giant's contraption."

I led the class to the now-resting copper head. I had lost the perp and discovered a new criminal group, but a useful lesson held more attraction for me. Plus, Gol and I had unlocked a new secret from the giants.

"You will have a heck of a report to produce," Zgouish said, looking the immobile snake up and down, impressed by the loops of mottled green hide.

"You bet," I said. "That should shut the ME's pothole for a while."

"Fancy that, a mere egg-layer (*Zgouish imitated a puff of scorn*) vanquishing the Green Snake!"

I was about to start explaining the nitty gritty of the metal-sticking when many stalks pointed up toward the green loops.

There was a bump sticking off the mantle of dirt and muck covering the green loops, three shell-lengths up. A round, mud-encrusted bump, its GGPD sign invisible, except when I extended my receptors and caught the signature scent.

I sent the ID call.

A few heartbeats after, a faint, tenuous puff answered. A fresh wave of relief washed over me, with less damage than the raging water.

Nool hadn't been squished under an overwhelming foot. His cracked shell must have fooled the giant into thinking he was dead.

*

LATER, the exhausted candidate told us his incredible story, munching on a tender dandelion leave.

After he had let go of Boon, the gushing water had pushed Nool against the snake's body. In an instinctive reflex, the candidate had stuck his foot to the plastic hide. He had travelled with the snake and witnessed the drenching visited on the Backyard district.

As his scent response reached the candidates, the whole class exploded in smelly cheers. So much for this afternoon lesson, I thought, one eyestalk arching towards my hunky partner.

This time, I was happy for the interruption.

THE END

Heartfelt Thanks

The first story of the GGPD, *Slime & Crime,* has been originally published in Fiction River 22, 2017, edited by WMG Publishing inc. under the direction of John Helfers.

If you enjoyed this story, share your impressions on your favorite platform like goodreads.com. This way, you gently guide more readers towards Michèle's stories.

Praise for Slime & Crime

"Laframboise does an excellent job of translating the rhythm and feel of the typical murder mystery into the realities of a snail's eye view. The story is clever and effectively conveys the point of view of the snails and the various limitations and talents available to them."

-- Robert Turner, Tangent

In the same series:

About the Author

WHEN NOT TRYING to initiate first contact with strange flora, Michèle Laframboise juggles her time between drawing comics and crafting stories.

A science-fiction lover since childhood, she has published 19 novels and more than 50 short stories, earning three Auroras and two Solaris awards.

Her works have appeared in *Solaris, Carmilla, Galaxies, Géante Rouge, Brin d'Éternité, Tesseracts, Fiction River, Compelling Science Fiction*, and *Abyss&Apex*. She has been translated into French, Italian and Russian.

Holding degrees in geography and engineering, Michèle uses her scientific background to create worlds filled with humor, invention and wonder.

Official website:
www.michele-laframboise.com
in French and English

Humoristic blog:
sundayartist.wordpress.com

Publisher's website:
www.echofictions.com

Wikipedia entry: Michèle Laframboise

For some news and amusing reading reviews, join
 Michele's happy band of readers!

http://michele-laframboise.com/fans

Other books by Michèle

Change or die!

Science-fiction / humor / First contact

Loongunis need constant fluctuations to thrive, while the strange-haired Earthmen hate the endless unstability.

When a sabotage impairs the shift engines of their traveling Box, the enforced immobility might drive all Loongunis mad...unless their translator can work out a solution!

Science fiction adventure at its best, a quirky 7000-word story told by multiple award-winning author Michèle Laframboise.

How to Think inside the Box
978-1-988339-40-5 (print)

Trapped in the most beautiful place on earth...

Humor / mystery / Ornithology

Equipped with her Sibley Guide and trusty binoculars, Amanda Byrd pursues the most elusive winged species. As she explores a beautiful canyon at dawn, Amanda discovers their lift sabotaged, trapping their group at the canyon's bottom.

Who did it, and why?

Our intrepid birdwatcher must find a way out before the sun turns the canyon into a mortal cauldron.

A short and spirited cozy mystery introducing the energetic Lady Byrd, written by Michèle Laframboise, multi-award winner author and amateur ornithologist.

Condor Cliff

ISBN 978-1-988339-08-5 (Print)

You won't forget Malak...

Child Labor/ Humanitarian / Sweatshops

Theo, a dispirited workplace humanitarian, audits a child worker at a cardboard factory, in a port city somewhere in Asia. He is impressed by young Malak's maturity and grit. When that boy, the same age as Theo's own son, disappears, he cannot let it rest. His quest for answers only raises more questions about the traps of structured help and acquired privilege.

An unsettling story quietly told by multiple awards-winning author Michèle Laframboise.

Cardboard Boy

ISBN 978-1-988339-22-1 (Print)

More sweet and bitter-sweet stories can be found on Echo-fictions.com/books

Friends' List

A story links every reader in a chain of friendship. Feel free to write your name before you give this book to someone close.

This is a unique feature of the printed edition!

_____

_____

_____

_____

_____

_____

_____

_____

_____

Yearning for more Stories?

Michèle Laframboise's full bibliography is enough to whet any reader's appetite! Visit her author site at:
michele-laframboise.com

New stories are brewing up constantly!

To get exclusive offers, curated book reviews, advanced information on events, join Michele's happy band of readers!

michele-laframboise.com/fans

As a very busy writer, Michèle won't send mail more often than once every two months.